THIS WALKER BOOK BELONGS TO:

_____

_____

_____

_____

THE ADVENTURES OF RAMA AND SITA

Prince Rama and his beloved Sita are the idols of the people of Ayodha. But the queen, Rama's stepmother, uses an old promise made to her by the king to disinherit the prince in favour of her own son, forcing Rama into exile with Sita and his brother Lakshman. Soon, in the dangerous Forest of Dandak, the three exiles encounter the wicked Ravana, King of the Demons, who plots to take Sita for his queen. In the mighty and magical struggle that follows, Rama receives valuable help from the wily Hanuman of the Monkey Kingdom. But Ravana is a very tricky and powerful enemy indeed...

WALKER STORYBOOKS

The Adventures of Rama and Sita
   by Ruskin Bond
Earthquake by Ruskin Bond
Hetty's First Fling by Diana Hendry
Our Horrible Friend by Hannah Cole
The Pepper Street Papers by Joan Smith
Robin Hood and Little John
   by Julian Atterton
Robin Hood and the Miller's Son
   by Julian Atterton
The Shape-Changer by Julian Atterton
Staples for Amos by Alison Morgan
We Three Kings from Pepper Street Prime
   by Joan Smith

The Adventures of
Rama and Sita

First published 1987 by
Julia MacRae Books
This edition published 1990 by
Walker Books Ltd, 87 Vauxhall Walk
London SE11 5HJ

Text © 1987 Ruskin Bond
Illustrations © 1987 Valerie Littlewood
Cover illustration by Valerie Littlewood

Printed in Great Britain by
Richard Clay Ltd, Bungay, Suffolk

British Library Cataloguing in Publication Data
Bond, Ruskin
The adventures of Rama and Sita.
I. Title
823'.914   PZ7
ISBN 0-7445-1445-2

The Adventures
of
Rama and Sita

Written by
RUSKIN BOND

Illustrated by
VALERIE LITTLEWOOD

WALKER BOOKS
LONDON

Contents

1 The Banishment of Rama

All through the warm summer night, the people of Ayodha, a kingdom in ancient India, worked to prepare their city for the morrow's celebrations, the coronation of their beloved Prince Rama. They hung gay lanterns from balconies and tree tops, and adorned the white temples of the city with banners and bamboo archways. They burned fragrant incense and strewed flowers upon all sides – roses, jasmine and marigolds. The people were in great good humour; there was not one who did not look forward to the celebrations, for Rama and his young wife, Sita, were the idols of the people's hearts.

7

Now, although Rama was to be crowned, his father, the King, was still alive. But the old King felt too tired and weak to perform his royal duties unaided. And so, from his three sons, Rama, Bharat, and Lakshman, he had chosen Rama, his first born, to share the throne with him.

Unfortunately for Rama, he had two dangerous enemies in the palace, and through no fault of his own. They were the Queen, his stepmother, and her old maidservant, Manthara, who was devoted to her and knew all her secrets. On this night of happy preparation, the two women were standing at a window in the palace, looking gloomily at the crowded streets below.

The Queen was bitter.

"If only these preparations were for my own son, Bharat, instead of for Rama, the King's favourite."

"And why shouldn't they be?" said Manthara. "Isn't Prince Bharat also beloved by his father, the King?"

"What do you mean?" asked the Queen. "Do

you think the King would place Bharat before
Rama at *my* request?"

"Stranger things than that have happened,"
said Manthara. And she recalled how, years
ago, the Queen had saved the King's life by
tending his wounds upon the battlefield, and
how, in return, the grateful King had sworn to
grant her two favours at any time that she
should ask for them.

"You have never claimed your rights,"
continued Manthara, "but the time has come
for those favours to be granted. Listen, my
Queen."

And drawing nearer to her mistress, she whispered a few words in her ear which made the Queen's eyes light up with excitement.

"Oh, wise Manthara," she cried. "I will do as you say." Dawn was now at hand, and there was no time to be lost as the celebrations would begin soon after sunrise. The Queen hurried to the King's apartment.

"My Lord," she said eagerly to the old King, who was reclining upon his couch. "Tell me this! Do you remember how I saved your life upon the battlefield long ago?"

"How could I forget your loving skill?" answered the King. "Nor have I forgotten the promise that I made you at that time. Have you come to ask for your two favours, my dear?"

The Queen bowed her head in assent.

"Ask those boons of me now," said the unsuspecting King, "and I swear by my dear son, Rama, that if it is in my power to grant your requests, they will be granted."

"Then," said the Queen in triumph, "grant me two things, my King. Let our son Bharat be crowned this day, and let Rama be banished to the Forest of Dandak for fourteen years."

The King nearly swooned with dismay and anger.

"What are you saying?" he cried in a shaking voice. "How can you be so treacherous! What wrong has Rama ever done you? No, such favours cannot be granted!"

"As you wish," replied the Queen calmly. "But you realise, of course, that your subjects will come to know of your broken promises to me. You will for ever be known throughout the lands of India as a King who failed to keep his solemn vow. You will be spoken of in scorn!"

The King knew that he was in his queen's power, for a ruler had always to be true to his word. And had he not vowed, in the name of his dear son, that he would grant the favours, cruel though they had proved to be? Vainly he begged the Queen to ask him any other favour, but she had set her mind on Rama's banishment. She thought that if Rama were sent to Dandak, a forest said to be full of demons and evil spirits, it was unlikely that he would return alive after fourteen years of exile.

Finding he could do nothing to make the Queen change her mind, the King resigned himself to his fate. With an aching heart, he entered the great audience-chamber in the palace where eager crowds were awaiting him.

To the amazement of everyone in the hall, the King announced that Bharat, not Rama, was to share his throne. There were cries of surprise and dismay from the people. Prince Rama, puzzled and unhappy, stepped forward. The excited crowd began to cheer him as he stood before the throne.

"What have I done, my father?" he asked with simple dignity. "Why have you dishonoured me?"

The King could no longer control his grief. Amidst bitter tears he spoke of his vow to the Queen – how her demands had to be granted, cruel and unjust though they might be.

"Not only must I deprive you of the throne," said the King despairingly, "but it is the desire of the Queen that you be banished to the Forest of Dandak for fourteen years."

When Bharat realized what had happened he

12

took Rama's hand and vowed that he would never take the throne from his brother.

But Rama, who had listened to his father's words in silence, now said:

"No, Bharat, the crown is yours. I must honour my father's promise. I will go to the Forest of Dandak, and not until fourteen years have passed will I return to the kingdom."

"You will not go alone," rang out a young woman's voice, and beautiful dark-eyed Sita, who until that moment had been overcome by grief and fear at the strange turn of events, now came and stood by her husband's side.

"I will share your exile," she said. "Alone here, I would surely die."

"But the Forest of Dandak is full of danger," said Rama gently. "You know well that Ravana, the King of the Demons, is said to haunt it with his followers. They are always looking for an opportunity to work their evil upon the good and the innocent."

"I must accompany you too, Rama," said Prince Lakshman, the King's third son, who had always been devoted to Rama. "I will help you to protect Sita."

Rama protested that he could not allow his wife and brother to endure the hardships of a forest life, but Sita and Lakshman begged to be allowed to accompany him. So at last he gave way to them. Then he turned to the King, and embracing the old man tenderly, he said:

"Farewell, Father. I do not blame you, for you have been the victim of the Queen's cunning."

So, amidst great sorrowing, Rama, Sita and Lakshman took leave of all those who loved them in the palace, and, after changing their royal robes for the plain clothes of forest folk, they set out towards the deep dark woods of Dandak which lay to the south of the kingdom.

2 In the Forest of Dandak

Scarcely had the three exiles left the palace, when the King fell into a coma from which all his doctors failed to revive him, and a few days later he was dead.

Now, thought the Queen, Bharat will be crowned at last.

But the Queen was doomed to disappointment, for Bharat refused to ascend the throne, saying that Rama must be brought back from the forest to take his rightful place as the King. The Queen begged her son not to throw away his chance of glory, but Bharat was determined to see justice done; so he journeyed to the Forest of Dandak and managed to overtake Rama and his companions.

Rama was deeply grieved to hear of his father's death, but he refused to listen to Bharat's pleas that he should now return to be crowned King.

"My father pledged his word that I should remain in exile for fourteen years," he said firmly, "and I will remain here in fulfilment of his vow."

"Then I will govern the people as your regent," said Bharat, "until the day when you return."

So Bharat took leave of the wanderers and, returning to the kingdom, he governed it with wisdom and justice. True to his word, he refused to be crowned, and he set a pair of Rama's wooden sandals upon the throne as a sign of his absent brother's authority.

The Queen had failed to make her son the real King, but neither she nor Manthara gave up hope, for they felt sure that Rama would never return from the Forest of Dandak.

Meanwhile the wanderers went deeper into the forest, living upon fruits and herbs. Some-

times they came across a tiny hermitage in which lived some holy man who gave them hospitality, otherwise they did not see a living soul in the forest. And although they were always on their guard against the Demon King Ravana and his followers, so far not a single evil spirit had appeared or troubled them.

One day they chanced to arrive at a little hermitage which was inhabited by an old priest of great repute.

The holy man welcomed them, and was astonished to hear that they had been in the forest for so long without being attacked by demons.

"Since I am a hermit, Ravana and his hosts do not bother to molest me," he said. "But I have often seen them lurking near this place, and I fear that you may be attacked by them. It may be that you have been destined by the gods to wage war upon these evil spirits who trouble the earth so much. I will give you my store of weapons."

Then, to Rama's delight, the priest presented him with a bow and a quiver full of an endless store of arrows. Lakshman received a golden-sheathed sword.

"These weapons once belonged to the great God Indra," said the priest, "and their aim is true and deadly. Now you may wander where you will, for the demons are afraid of the arrows and this sword."

As Rama touched his bow with loving fingers, he solemnly vowed to himself that he would rid the world of all evil.

They rested for a while at the hermitage, then Rama said, "Oh, best and wisest among the

sages, please direct us to some pleasant place, where we may spend the remaining years of our exile."

"Seek the Vale of Plenty," advised the holy man. "It is a pleasant, fertile glade where you may live in comfort and peace."

So the wanderers took leave of him and continued on their journey, armed with their precious weapons.

Following the sage's directions, they soon reached the Vale of Plenty, which was a truly beautiful, tranquil spot. There were blossoming magnolias and mango trees laden with fruit. Peacocks danced in the forest clearings, and many-hued parrots flew swiftly from tree to tree. A little stream of fresh water wound its way through the glade.

"Let us remain here," cried Sita eagerly, so the brothers set to work to build her a small dwelling.

This was soon done, and Sita was as delighted with her new home as if it had been a palace. The walls of the hut were made of hardened earth instead of marble, and, in the place of gleaming columns, pillars of bamboo supported the thatched roof. They were happy in this simple abode, and as the years slipped peacefully by, Rama felt convinced that the demons would never trouble them. Had not the sage given them protection with his magic weapons?

He was soon to discover his mistake, and to learn from bitter experience that magic weapons alone were not enough to protect the good and innocent from the evil spells of King Ravana.

3   The Demon King

Ravana, the King of the Demons, was
determined to do something about the royal
forest-dwellers, since he was the sworn enemy
of gods and virtuous mortals. He knew that the
sage had given them magic weapons, and
realized that it would be dangerous for him to
attack the brothers openly. He had to find some
way of slaying them by stealth. So he constantly
lurked unseen near the Vale of Plenty, in the
hope of meeting the brothers unarmed; but as
yet he had not caught sight of them without
their weapons.

One evening while Ravana was watching
them from a distance, he had an idea which

23

made him very pleased with himself.

Sita is most beautiful, he thought, and she is dearer to Rama than his very life. I will not waste time trying to kill the proud Prince. Instead I will steal his most cherished possession. Yes, Sita shall be mine!

The longer Ravana thought about his scheme, the more it delighted him, although he knew that the capture of Sita would be no easy task, for neither Rama nor Lakshman ever left her unguarded. Still, Ravana had all the aids of sorcery at his command, and he decided to ask the help of his cousin, Marichi, who was said to be the most cunning of all the demon race.

Marichi lived alone in a distant part of the forest, so Ravana sent for his chariot.

The chariot was a golden vehicle drawn by two fierce-looking asses with goblins' heads. Not only could this strange car roll over the ground with great swiftness, but it was also able to fly through the air like an aeroplane. Ravana stepped inside his car and flew to the most gloomy part of the forest, where Marichi was studying the arts of magic.

24

"Greetings, my kinsman!" said Ravana. "I have come to you for help. Do you know that Prince Rama has dared to enter this forest with Sita, his wife, and his brother, Lakshman?"

"Yes, Ravana," said Marichi gloomily. "But take care. Do not molest them, for I have a strong feeling that they will bring trouble upon us."

Ravana laughed at his cousin's words, but Marichi remained serious.

"I think the gods themselves have sent this powerful Prince to destroy us," he said. "Did you know, cousin, that the magic arrows of Indra are in his possession?"

"Yes, I know," answered Ravana, "and that is why I do not plan to fight him. But listen! What I propose to do will injure him more than death."

Then Ravana told his cousin how he planned to carry Sita away to his enchanted palace upon the distant island of Lanka.

"She shall become my queen," he said. "And Rama will look for her in vain, for no mortal can cross the seas which divide Lanka from this land."

"You shall get no help from me, cousin," said
Marichi firmly, "for I know that disaster lies in
store for us if we do anything to harm Rama.
Let Sita be, I beg you. Go back and find
another, more beautiful bride."

But Ravana was not to be put off by his
cousin, and as he knew that he would never be
able to carry out his scheme without the aid of
Marichi, he raised his sword and shouted,
"Refuse to help me, and you shall die!"

Seeing that Ravana was in deadly earnest,
Marichi gave in, saying, "It is better for me to
be killed by Rama than by you. At least then I
would lose my life to an enemy."

Ravana was overjoyed and embraced his
cousin. "Now you are again my dear Marichi!"
And stepping inside the chariot, they set out
for the Vale of Plenty.

4   The Golden Gazelle

Rama and his companions were enjoying the
cool dawn of a summer morning, before the
sun rose in fiery splendour and forced them to
seek shelter. Lakshman wandered a little way
from the glade in search of fresh fruit, while
Rama and Sita busied themselves with
household tasks.

"Oh, look!" cried Sita suddenly, pointing to a
young gazelle which had just bounded into
sight. "Such a beautiful little creature! How
graceful it is – and how lovely its shining coat.
Like living gold! I wish it were mine."

"And what would you do with it?" asked
Rama.

"I would make it my playfellow," she answered wistfully. "And when the long years of our exile have passed, I will take it back with me to our kingdom."

"You shall have your wish," said Rama, and he set off in pursuit of the gazelle. But the timid little creature sprang back and hid itself among the trees.

Sita gave a cry of disappointment, and the gazelle reappeared, only to elude Rama's grasp once more by springing still further into the forest.

"I will catch the animal for you, never fear," said Rama, and called out to his brother: "Lakshman! Come and look after Sita while I catch this gazelle."

Lakshman returned to the glade to remain with Sita; and Rama, picking up his bow and arrows, ran swiftly after the gazelle, which was darting about in a tantalizing fashion. First it led Rama through some thickets, then it rushed far into the forest. It went so far that the Prince grew hot and weary. But he would not give up the pursuit.

"This is the first thing Sita has asked for since we came to live in the forest," he told himself. "If it is in my power to grant it, she shall have her wish."

On bounded the gazelle, now coming near Rama, now hiding itself, until at last, when the Prince realized how far he had travelled from the Vale of Plenty, he began to feel uneasy.

This is not the way of an innocent wild creature, he thought. What if it be some trick of the demons to lure me away from Sita! It's a good thing Lakshman is with her.

Once more the gazelle darted towards him, then, as Rama raised his hand, it sprang away.

"No," said the puzzled Prince, "even if I were to capture this animal, it would not be a fit playmate for Sita. So I will kill the creature and take her its golden coat."

Rama drew his bow and let fly one of his magic arrows. Immediately the animal fell to the ground, and Rama felt a pang of remorse for having injured so beautiful a creature.

And then a strange thing happened.

The gazelle slowly began to change its shape.

To Rama's astonishment it took on the form of a demon with a deadly wound in his side.

The demon was Marichi who, by means of his sorcery, had turned himself into a gazelle hoping to lure both Rama and Lakshman from the side of Sita.

Half of the demon's work had been done, for here was Rama, far from his wife. But, as he looked upon the Prince with eyes of hatred, Marichi made one last effort to complete the task that Ravana had set him.

"Help, Lakshman, help!" he shouted in a voice which was exactly like the voice of Rama. Then the demon fell back lifeless, whilst Rama stood by in wonder and dismay.

Marichi's dying cry had echoed through the forest, as far as the Vale of Plenty. At the terrible sound, Sita looked at Lakshman in terror.

"It was the voice of Rama!" she cried. "He is in danger. Go quickly to him, Lakshman!"

"No, Sita," said Lakshman gravely. "I cannot leave you, for I gave my word to Rama that I would remain with you during his absence."

"Oh, do go, I beg of you," cried Sita, almost in tears. "Hurry, brother, or you will be too late!"

"Calm yourself," said Lakshman. "It was the voice of some evil spirit in the forest. Why should Rama call for help? He can protect himself with the magic arrows."

But Sita refused to be comforted. "Are you frightened?" she cried bitterly. "Are you afraid to help your brother?"

She continued to taunt him until at last Lakshman agreed to go. Telling her not to leave the hut no matter what happened, he hurried away in the direction from which the mysterious cry had come.

5   The Capture of Sita

Sita was not afraid of being left alone, but she
could not bear the thought that Lakshman
might arrive too late to help Rama. She blamed
herself for the foolish whim that had sent Rama
off in quest of the gazelle.

The moments passed, and each one seemed
like an hour to Sita as she crouched by the hut,
watching every movement of the trees, and
listening intently for the sound of footsteps.
Presently she heard a rustling in the bushes,
and she sprang to her feet. A man stood there.
He was neither Rama nor Lakshman, only an
old hermit with bowed shoulders and a flowing
white beard.

As the old man drew near, Sita noticed with a pang of fear that a change had suddenly stolen over the forest. Until that moment the sun had shone and the trees had been noisy with bird song. Now there was nothing to be heard. Not a leaf rustled. The sky was suddenly overcast.

"May I rest here for a while?" asked the stranger in a feeble voice. "I am tired and hungry."

"I will bring you food and water," said Sita timidly, and the old man thanked her. His gaze was steady, his eyes curiously bright and piercing.

"Who are you?" he asked. "And why do you live in this dangerous and lonely forest? Your beauty and grace should adorn a palace, not this rude hut."

Sita told him how she had chosen to share the exile of her husband, and when she explained that her fancy for the gazelle had caused both Rama and Lakshman to leave her on her own, the old man smiled to himself. Then he stood upright, and at once a change took place in him – his shrunken height increased to a mighty stature, his aged face grew youthful, bold and mocking, and his hermit's robe fell to the ground, revealing the regal clothes beneath. It was none other than the King of the Demons who stood there – terrible Ravana himself!

Sita drew back with a cry of terror.

"Have no fear, Sita, I will not harm you," said Ravana in a friendly manner. "You must know that I am Ravana, and I have come to make you my queen. You will live in my beautiful palace on the island of Lanka, and your days will be full of delight."

He held out his arms, but Sita shrank from him, crying out: "Do you not know that I am the wife of Prince Rama!"

"Rama will never return to you," said Ravana. "My cousin, Marichi, has dealt with him. It was Marichi himself who took the form of a gazelle in order to lure Rama deep into the forest."

Sita did not know whether to believe him or not; but on Ravana's face she saw nothing but triumph.

"You will come with me," he said.

His magic chariot appeared, and he forced her into it. As the chariot soared upwards, Sita felt that all was lost.

"You can carry me away," she cried desperately, "but I will never become your queen. I will remain faithful to Rama whether he is alive or dead."

Ravana's only reply was to urge his steeds to travel faster, for he saw in the distance a dark speck coming towards him, and he was afraid that already someone was in pursuit.

Nearer came this strange object, and Ravana recognized that it was Jatai, King of the Vultures, who had always been an enemy of the demon race.

"Stop, Ravana!" cried the great bird as he soared above the chariot. "Where are you taking her?"

"Oh, good bird, help me!" called Sita. "I am the wife of Prince Rama, and this cruel King has captured me by cunning and force."

"Let her go!" commanded Jatai.

"Out of my way, ugly vulture," said Ravana

scornfully.

Jatai hurled himself fiercely upon Ravana, but the Demon King's spear was thrust deep into the vulture's side.

"Sita, I cannot help you now," moaned the wounded bird. "May the Gods protect you!" And gasping with pain, noble Jatai sank down to the earth far below.

Ravana laughed with triumph, and the chariot floated on, above plains and hills, and over a great mountain. Sita caught a glimpse of some huge monkeys moving about on the mountain. Acting on a sudden impulse, she loosened her scarf and necklace and let them fall into the hands of the creatures below.

Onward flew the chariot, over villages and cities, until at last it neared the sea coast. Then away it flew over the stormy ocean, to the Emerald Isle of Lanka, where Sita was destined to spend many sad and lonely years.

6 Hanuman to the Rescue

After the strange death of the demon, Marichi,
Rama hurried back to the Vale of Plenty, but
before he had gone far he met Lakshman coming
towards him.

"Where is Sita?" called Rama. "You have left
her unguarded!"

Lakshman began to explain what had
happened but Rama cried out: "Oh Lakshman,
we have been tricked! Come quickly, for there
is evil about in the forest."

They rushed back, calling for Sita, but when
they reached the hut they found it empty.

"The demons have stolen her," said Rama,
and though the brothers continued to search,

they could find no trace of her until they discovered the vulture, Jatai, bleeding to death from the wound in his side.

"Are you searching for Sita, the wife of Rama?" asked the bird, raising his head with an effort. "I received this wound in her defence. Ravana took her away in his chariot . . ."

"Where – tell us where!" pleaded Rama. "In which direction did they go?"

"Southwards," whispered the dying bird. "Towards the great mountain – take help from the Monkey King!" And then the great bird died.

In order to show their gratitude and respect for Jatai, Rama and Lakshman lit a fire and gave the noble bird an honourable funeral. Then, with hope still alive in their hearts, they set out to find the mountain that lay to the south.

For many months they wandered through heavy forest, but at last they reached open country once more. Beyond the wide plain which stretched before them, they could see a lofty mountain in the distance.

41

They hurried towards it, but just as they were about to start climbing, a huge monkey appeared from a dense thicket to bar their way.

"Stay where you are!" said the great animal fiercely. "I am Hanuman, the Minister of the Monkey King who lives upon this mountain. Tell me why you are here."

In spite of his fierce appearance and rough manner, there was something kindly in Hanuman's face. Rama felt instinctively that he had found a friend, and began to tell his story.

To his joy he soon learned that, not only had Hanuman seen the chariot of Ravana flying southward, but that a woman in the car had flung down her ornaments, which had actually fallen into Hanuman's hands. He showed Rama these treasures, and the Prince at once recognized Sita's silken scarf and glittering necklace.

"Perhaps our king can help you," said Hanuman. "Come, follow me to my master."

The Monkey King was pleased to see Rama and Lakshman. Troubled by the demons as well as by a treacherous brother, he was glad to have the Princes as his allies.

While they made plans to raise an army large enough to vanquish the demon race, Hanuman decided to make an expedition of his own. He would spy out the land and locate Ravana's island fortress and try to discover Sita's exact whereabouts.

Upon the top of a mountain he found an old vulture called Sampati, the brother of that good Jatai who had lost his life in the defence of Sita. Sampati had singed his wings in a bold attempt to fly over the sun, and he was now resting to recover from his injuries; but he told Hanuman that before he had fallen from the dizzy heights to which he had ascended, he had seen the chariot of Ravana coming down on the shores of the island of Lanka.

"There was someone struggling in the chariot," said Sampati. "That must have been Sita. But how will you rescue her? The island is surrounded by dangerous seas which only Ravana and his demons have been able to cross."

Hanuman decided to visit Lanka by himself,

to discover how strong the demons were, and how Sita could be rescued. So, telling no one, he slipped away to the sea coast. But he found that Sampati's warning was only too true. Stormy seas divided the island from the mainland.

Hanuman did not give up easily. He had always been famed for his great prowess in leaping, and he decided to make an attempt to spring over the raging waters.

He climbed to the top of a rock, gave one flying leap, and found himself upon the shore of Lanka.

7 Hanuman's Tail of Fire

Hanuman looked about him, and was astonished to find that the place was so beautiful. The soft grass at his feet was studded with flowers, the trees around him were covered with spring blossoms. In the distance shone the white walls of a great city.

He lingered outside the city until it grew dark; then, afraid that his huge size might attract attention, he changed himself into a tiny monkey and nimbly scaled the city walls.

It did not take him long to find Ravana's palace. He went from window to window, but he could not see Sita in any of the apartments. Having refused time and again to marry Ravana,

46

she had been made a prisoner in a solitary part of the palace grounds where she was guarded by several cruel demons who missed no opportunity to tease and torment her.

Wandering in the palace gardens, Hanuman glimpsed a small white pavilion, half hidden in a grove of trees. He peeped through a window, and could hardly hold back a cry of joy, for there lay the most beautiful woman he had ever seen, and he knew that Sita was found at last. Her sorrow had made her pale and thin, but her goodness and beauty could not be destroyed.

He waited until she came to the window, and then, in a gentle voice, he whispered, "Rama."

Sita gave a start, but seeing no one except a tiny monkey before her, she thought she must have dreamed the sound of Rama's name.

"Rama," whispered Hanuman again, and this time he held out a golden ring which Rama had given him, and upon which the name of the Prince was engraved.

At the sight of this token from her husband, Sita became very excited; but Hanuman begged her to control herself, for, should her demon guards discover him, his plans for her rescue might fail. But the guards paid no attention to the little chattering monkey, and he told Sita that he would bring Rama to her rescue without delay. Already, he told her, an army was preparing to march on Lanka.

Unfortunately, as he was leaving the city, Hanuman could not resist the temptation to trouble Ravana. Changing back to his natural size, and tearing up huge trees and stones, he hurled them at the walls of Ravana's palace. He was enjoying himself so much that he failed to notice that demons were rushing to attack him from all directions. When at last he became aware of the danger, he seized a marble pillar as a weapon and leaped upon the roof of Ravana's palace.

"Long live Rama!" he cried, laying about with his marble club. "I am Hanuman, friend of Rama, here to bring ruin upon Ravana and his demons!"

He took another leap, hoping that it would land him beyond the reach of his enemies, but he was struck by an arrow and fell to the

ground, surrounded by hordes of shrieking, vengeful demons.

Hanuman was only slightly wounded, but he was now completely in the power of his enemies. They put him in chains and dragged him before Ravana.

"A quick death would be too small a punishment for this intruder," declared Ravana. "Set the spying ape alight, and let him slowly burn to death."

The demons brought strips of cotton soaked in oil and bound them round Hanuman's tail; then they set fire to these rags and stood by to gloat over him.

When Sita was told what was happening, she offered a prayer to the God of Fire: "Oh, Agni! If there be any goodness in me, be cool to Hanuman. Do not hurt him."

The rags soaked in oil burned brightly, but the fire did not hurt Hanuman. He burst his bonds with a mighty effort, and leaped away from his astonished enemies, lashing his tail to and fro and setting fire to everything that it touched. He jumped from one tall building to

50

another, setting fire to them. In a little while a strong breeze began to blow and half the city was in flames.

Hanuman went to the sea and, plunging in, put out the fire in his tail.

Then he rushed back to the pavilion to warn Sita to keep far away from the burning palace. Returning to the seashore, he crossed the ocean with another powerful leap, and went in search of Rama.

8   The Battle Begins

Rama was overjoyed when he heard that Sita
was alive and well. The Monkey King was quite
willing to give Rama a large army, and the
monkeys came forward in thousands, excited at
the chance of attacking their old enemies the
demons. But when this mighty force, led by
Rama, Lakshman and Hanuman, reached the
southern coast, they found that the ocean was
still raging and it seemed impossible for the
army to cross over to Lanka. Only Hanuman
was capable of leaping over the waters.

"A bridge must be built for our forces," said
Rama. "Let the most powerful monkeys throw
great rocks and tree trunks into the ocean, and
you will see that in this way a causeway will be

made for our army."

Thousands of great monkeys immediately set to work. They uprooted trees and tore huge rocks from the cliffs, and when these objects were thrown into the sea, they began to form a bridge which in five days' time reached as far as the shores of Lanka.

Then during the night, Rama led his forces over the causeway. They landed in safety at Lanka, where they encamped at some distance from the city.

Ravana had seen the approach of the enemy from a watch-tower in his palace. When he saw the strength of the monkey army, he was filled with dismay. Rousing his men, he ordered them to make ready for battle without delay, and at daybreak the Demon King marched out of the city with thousands of his fierce demon warriors.

Rama's forces were armed with great stones and uprooted tree-trunks, which they hurled with all their might against the enemy. But, although countless demons were killed in this way, it seemed as if their ranks could not be

thinned. The brave monkeys suffered much from the poisoned spears and arrows which the demons used.

At the end of the first day's fighting, Lakshman was badly wounded. But Hanuman was at hand to apply healing herbs to the Prince's wounds, and Lakshman was soon able to take part in the battle again.

For many days and nights the fighting continued, and at first it seemed as if Ravana and his demons would triumph; but gradually the tide of fortune began to turn in favour of Rama. One by one, Ravana's most powerful warriors fell before the magic arrows of Rama. In desperation the Demon King decided to force his giant brother to enter the fray.

9 Ravana Defeated

Now this giant brother was the strongest of all the demons, an enormous monster of a fellow! Unfortunately he had always been a great source of trouble to Ravana. When he moved, his huge clumsy limbs were apt to cause much damage to buildings and gardens, and his appetite was so great that it could never be satisfied. As a result, Ravana had forced the poor giant to pass his days in slumber, and only twice a year was he allowed to wake up and enjoy a few hours' freedom.

It was not the proper season for the demon giant to be awakened, but Ravana gave orders that he should be roused instantly and told of the desperate plight of the demon armies.

The awakening of the giant was something of a problem, for though the demons clapped their hands and shouted, he did not move; nor did his peaceful snoring cease when trumpets were sounded in his ears. Elephants and camels were then brought into the giant's massive apartment, and made to trumpet and bellow, but still he slept. It was not until the animals were driven over his great body that he stirred and asked in a drowsy voice, "Why am I disturbed before the appointed time?"

The demons hastily explained why they had been forced to rouse him, and the giant muttered: "Ravana has been foolish to anger Rama and these monkeys. But to please my brother I will march against them."

So after he had refreshed himself with great quantities of food and wine, the demon giant stumbled out to battle.

The appearance of this terrible giant caused quite a panic amongst the monkeys, thousands of whom were killed as he went crashing through their ranks. But Rama advanced

fearlessly with the magic bow which the old sage had given him. And, to the joy of his followers, he sent an arrow right through the heart of this terrible opponent.

The giant fell to earth, crushing countless demons beneath his dead body.

But now the greatest trial of Rama was to come.

Ravana hastily armed himself with all the deadly weapons at his command and rushed upon the Prince with howls of rage and defiance. Rama managed to withstand the poisoned darts and spears of his enemy; but it seemed as if his own magic weapons had lost their power. Arrow after arrow he aimed at Ravana, yet the Demon King remained unharmed.

At last, just as his strength was beginning to fail him, victory came to Rama.

One arrow, swifter and more powerful than the others, found its way to the heart of Ravana. The Demon King fell from his chariot and lay dead on the battlefield.

*

With the death of their King, the demons lost heart, and, laying down their arms, they surrendered to Hanuman's forces. Meanwhile, Prince Rama had entered the city in search of his wife.

Sita was alone in her pavilion, for her terrified guards had long since fled the city. When she heard the sound of footsteps she looked up in fear lest Ravana had returned, but catching sight of Rama, she rushed forward and fell into his arms with tears of joy.

At first Rama and Sita could hardly believe that their long separation was at an end. And the happy thought came to the Prince that his beloved wife had been found at the very moment when his sentence of banishment was over.

When good Hanuman heard this, he rushed off to inform Prince Bharat that Rama and Sita were about to return to the kingdom. The defeated demons brought out a wonderful chariot which they presented to the Prince and his princess.

Then Rama and Sita stepped into the flower-

covered car drawn by swans, and took leave of
Lanka for ever. The swans flew through the air
with the flower-chariot, and brought them
swiftly to their kingdom, where they found the
people rejoicing at the news of their safe return.

Prince Bharat was delighted to hand over the
rule of the kingdom to his brother, and the
coronation of Rama and Sita took place at last.

There was no jealous soul to spoil the ceremony this time, for the Queen's maidservant was dead, and the Queen, sorry for what she had done, had asked and received Rama's forgiveness.

Lakshman received many honours, and good Hanuman returned to his mountain home, with gifts for himself and the Monkey King. But what Hanuman valued far more than gold and jewels was the love and gratitude which Rama and Sita and their people would always feel towards him. And even today Hanuman is revered along with the other gods, goddesses and heroes of ancient India.

Ruskin Bond lives in Mussoorie in the Himalayas and over the years he has heard and collected many Indian legends. He has also written many original stories of his own, set in India, including the Walker Storybook *Earthquake*, and *Getting Granny's Glasses*, *The Eyes of the Eagle*, *Cricket for the Crocodile*, *Ghost Trouble* and *Snake Trouble* (all published by Julia MacRae Books). He is a former winner of the John Llewellyn Rhys Award for a first novel.

Here are some more WALKER STORYBOOK titles for you to enjoy

We Three Kings From
PEPPER STREET PRIME

by Joan Smith

(black and white illustrations by
Nicole Goodwin)

Pepper Street Primary's
Christmas concert is
never a dull affair –
chaotic, yes, but dull,
no. This year, with the
lively Em playing the Virgin
Mary and her football-mad younger
brother in the supportng
cast, the production looks
like being even
more colourful
and chaotic than
usual!

A WALKER STORYBOOK

The Pepper Street Papers

by Joan Smith

(black and white illustrations
by Nicole Goodwin)

When the Head announces
that Pepper Street Primary
may have to close, Sam
and his class decide
to commit the school to
floppy disc. Meanwhile,
Sam's sister Em appoints
herself official school
photographer. The result,
as ever, is chaos!

A WALKER STORYBOOK

EARTHQUAKE

by Ruskin Bond

(black and white illustrations by
Valerie Littlewood)

"What do you do when there's
an earthquake?" asks Rakesh.
Everyone in the Burman
household has their own
ideas, but when the tremors
begin and everything starts to shake and
quake, to crack and
crumble, they are
taken by surprise...

A WALKER STORYBOOK

ROBIN HOOD

and *LITTLE JOHN*

by Julian Atterton

(black and white illustrations by
John Dillow)

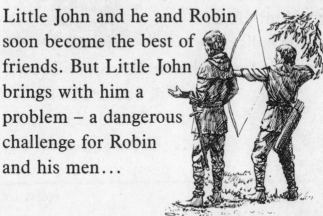

One day, when walking
in the forest, Robin
Hood encounters a
huge stranger – and
ends up in the river!
The man is, of course,
Little John and he and Robin
soon become the best of
friends. But Little John
brings with him a
problem – a dangerous
challenge for Robin
and his men...

A WALKER STORYBOOK

ROBIN HOOD

and the
MILLER'S SON

by Julian Atterton

(black and white illustrations by
John Dillow)

When Much the Miller's son is
seized by the cruel Sir
Guy of Gisburn,
Robin Hood is
determined to
save him. To do
so, he enlists the
help of Marian, her father, Sir Gilbert,
and Will Scarlet. But when
the day of his daring rescue
comes, Robin's greatest ally
is a giant shepherd called
John...

A WALKER STORYBOOK

Our Horrible Friend

by Hannah Cole
(black and white illustrations by Julie Stiles)

Like Diane and Jenny, Poppy lives with her mum and visits her dad on Saturdays.

But when Poppy and her mum start visiting Diane and Jenny's dad on Saturdays, the two sisters are not at all pleased. And this is just the first of several surprises...

A WALKER STORYBOOK

Hetty's First Fling

by Diana Hendry
(black and white illustrations by
Nicole Goodwin)

Great Uncle Fergus's
seventy-fifth
birthday party
means a trip
to the Isle of Skye for the Mungoe family –
and, for Hetty in particular, a very special
knees up indeed!

A WALKER STORYBOOK

STAPLES FOR AMOS

by Alison Morgan

(black and white illustrations
by Charles Front)

When Mum forgets to
buy staples for Amos
to mend the fence of the
bullock field, Daley acts quickly to try
and save her from the
anger of the old farm
worker. But his action
leads him into danger...

"A story of courage and determination...
A simple, imaginative and rather
moving tale."
British Book News

A WALKER STORYBOOK

MORE WALKER PAPERBACKS

For You to Enjoy

Name _____

Address _____

_____

_____